Great Explorers

MERIWETHER LEWIS AND WILLIAM CLARK

Stephen Krensky

A Crabtree Crown Book

Crabtree Publishing
crabtreebooks.com

School-to-Home Support for Caregivers and Teachers

This appealing book is designed to teach students about core subject areas. Students will build upon what they already know about the subject, and engage in topics that they want to learn more about. Here are a few guiding questions to help readers build their comprehensions skills. Possible answers appear here in red.

Before Reading:

What do I know about this topic?

- *I know that Lewis and Clark were American explorers that led an expedition through the West.*
- *I know that Lewis and Clark were aided by Sacagawea, a Shoshone woman.*

What do I want to learn about this topic?

- *I want to learn more about the route and difficulties that Lewis and Clark faced on their expedition.*
- *I want to learn more about how Lewis and Clark worked with Native Americans such as Sacagawea.*

During Reading:

I'm curious to know...

- *I'm curious to know how Lewis and Clark made decisions about where to take their expedition.*
- *I'm curious to know if Meriwether Lewis took on a leadership role over William Clark.*

How is this like something I already know?

- *I know that many Americans were sent on expeditions to explore the West.*
- *I know that the Louisiana Purchase greatly expanded the United States.*

After Reading:

What was the author trying to teach me?

- *I think the author was trying to teach me that Lewis and Clark relied on Sacagawea's skills.*
- *I think the author was trying to teach me about how Americans learned more about the geography of the West.*

How did the photographs and captions help me understand more?

- *The pictures helped me understand the tools and transportation methods used by Lewis and Clark.*
- *The map of the Louisiana Purchase reminded me of how large the land area was and how it encompassed many of todays current states.*

Table of Contents

Chapter 1:
Where to Go Next?

Which way should they go next?

That was the question facing Meriwether Lewis and William Clark on June 2, 1805. The two explorers were leading an expedition sent out by President Thomas Jefferson to explore the Louisiana Purchase.

Thomas Jefferson

The United States had paid France 15 million dollars for this vast **expanse** of land in 1803. It stretched from the Mississippi River westward to the Rocky Mountains and north to present-day Canada. It was 828,000 square miles (2,140,000 sq. km.) of fields, plains, forests, mountains, rivers, lakes, and prairies that, unlike the **Indigenous** peoples who already lived there, Jefferson and others from the United States didn't know much about.

Lewis and Clark were going to change all that.

Louisiana Purchase

Full-size replica of a keelboat at the Lewis & Clark State Park, on an inlet of the Missouri River in Onawa, Iowa

The Corps of Discovery Expedition, as it was formally called, had left St. Louis, Missouri a year earlier, on May 14, 1804. About 45 men, including soldiers, hunters, an interpreter, and a boat crew departed on a keelboat heading west on the Missouri River.

They carried with them a wide variety of supplies. There were scientific instruments—compasses, a **sextant**, a telescope, and a **chronometer**. They also had medical supplies for emergencies, blankets, ropes, pots and pans, weapons, tools, as well as books on plants, geography, and astronomy.

At that time, the origin of the Missouri River was still unknown. But the hope was that after 1,000 miles (1,609 km) or more, it would join up with the Columbia River in the Oregon territory. The Columbia River was already known to flow into the Pacific Ocean. If the Missouri River met up with the Columbia River, this would connect the Pacific Ocean to the various rivers back east.

Missouri River in North Dakota

At a speed of about 15 miles (24 km) a day, the expedition had spent the summer and fall of 1804 traveling through the future states of Kansas, Iowa, Nebraska, South Dakota, and North Dakota.

Meriwether looking out from rock

With winter coming, Lewis and Clark had ordered a fort to be built in early November near present-day Washburn, North Dakota. They named it Fort Mandan in honor of the Mandan tribe that lived in the area. The fort was shaped like a triangle and was protected by a 16 foot (4.8 m) tall picket fence on all three sides. Small huts lined the inside of the fence, each with its own chimney.

Around that time, they met and hired the French-Canadian trapper Toussaint Charbonneau to be an interpreter. Charbonneau was traveling with his Shoshone wife, Sacagawea. She had been captured from her village and sold, along with another woman, to Charbonneau. She was 15 years old and had just given birth to a son when she became part of the Lewis and Clark expedition along with her husband.

Sacagawea proved to be enormously helpful in the next part of the trip. She helped collect edible plants and **negotiated** with different tribes for supplies and horses. Her presence on the expedition also helped reinforce to others that its intentions were peaceful.

Sacagawea with Lewis and Clark

The next spring, on April 7, the Corps had started out from Fort Mandan. Eight weeks later, they found themselves facing the fork in the river.

It was not clear if Lewis and Clark would draw from past experience to help them make their decision. Meriwether Lewis had been born in Virginia in 1774 and later became a captain in the United States Army. Most recently, he had been the

Meriwether Lewis

personal secretary to President Jefferson for four years.

William Clark was four years older than Lewis. He had also been born in Virginia, but his family had moved to Kentucky when he was 15. He too had served in the army, having first joined his state militia at 19.

The two men had met years earlier and become friends when Lewis had served under Clark in the 1790s during campaigns in Kentucky, Indiana, and Ohio. After Jefferson chose Lewis to lead the expedition, Lewis had quickly asked Clark to join him.

William Clark

Chapter 2: A Big Decision

The two leaders both thought that the south fork, with its clearer water, was the right one to take. But many members of the Corps believed the muddier river heading north looked more like a continuation of the Missouri they already knew so well.

Rather than simply order everyone to go south, Lewis and Clark recommended that both branches be explored for a distance in the hope of discovering some new information. Going north revealed nothing new, but the landscape in the southern direction matched reports of what was supposed to lie ahead. Given this information, they chose to go south at a place that would later be called Decision Point.

Decision Point

The Lewis and Clark Expedition camped at the confluence of the Marias and the Missouri rivers on June 2–12, 1805. The long stay allowed the group to rest and contemplate a dilemma. Which river flowed over the "Great Falls" described by the Mandan Indians?

Information provided by the Mandans had been reliable to this point. But finding the Marias River was a surprise. The correct decision would lead the expedition to the best route across the Rocky Mountains. A wrong decision could strand them unprepared for a potentially deadly winter.

Lewis led a small party up the Marias; Clark, the Missouri. The Missouri was clear with a rocky bed, characteristics of rivers that have recently emerged from the mountains. The Marias was swollen and muddy from spring runoff. They chose the Missouri. The captains' judgment was rewarded the next day, June 13, when the falls were discovered.

NATIONAL CONSERVATION LANDS

Upper Missouri River Breaks
National Monument

15

Chapter 3: Bridging a Gap

Choosing the south fork, however, soon brought them a new problem. A really big one. Almost two weeks later, at the site of what later would be appropriately called Great Falls, Montana, they found themselves facing a giant waterfall. It was 80 feet (24 m) high and 900 feet (274 m) wide. They had heard something about a great waterfall before, but knowing it was coming and seeing it in person were not the same thing. Clearly, there was no way they could ride across it. They would have to go around, carrying all their baggage and boats overland until they could safely put them back in the river.

However, even this solution was not so simple. Further investigation showed that this great waterfall was not alone. Four more waterfalls, though smaller, stretched out over a distance of 18 miles (29 km). To safely continue their journey, they were going to have to transport everything beyond all five of the falls in their way.

Black Eagle Falls, Great Falls, Montana

Lugging their supplies in a **portage** of this length would have been difficult in the best of conditions. But their route was hilly and dotted with prickly pear cactus. The fierce summer heat was only interrupted by even fiercer storms, some of which contained hail big enough to draw blood from exposed arms and legs.

And that wasn't all. While the men busied themselves making crude carts from cottonwood trees, they were menaced by pests, both large and small. The grizzly bears, at least, could usually be easily seen or heard. The **gnats** and mosquitoes, on the other hand, were harder to fend off. As Lewis would later comment, "it is impossible to sleep a moment without being defended against the attacks of these most tormenting of all insects."

Chapter 4:
The Journey Continues

31 days later, on July 4, 1805, they finally finished the portage. Lewis and Clark had planned on delays that might set them back a day or two. But they had never expected a delay that would last a month. The loss of time mattered a lot because even in the middle of summer, they were always aware of where they might end up spending the coming winter. They did not want that to be in the wrong place.

However, given their accomplishment and the fact that it was Independence Day, they decided the group truly had something to celebrate. And so, they held a party with drinking and dancing that lasted far into the night.

Good luck at least returned the next month when the expedition met up with members of the Shoshone tribe. The group was amazed to find that the chief of this tribe was Sacagawea's brother, Cameahwait. With Sacagawea herself doing the interpreting, the expedition was able to trade for enough horses to continue traveling over the mountains to come.

Lewis and Clark interacting with Native Americans

One of the main goals that Jefferson had set forth was to develop peaceful relations with the various tribes Lewis and Clark were likely to meet. To reach this goal, the expedition had taken both time and energy to establish friendships, if possible, with the Native Americans they encountered. Among the tribes they met were the Shoshone, the Mandan, the Chinook, and the Sioux. Representatives from these tribes were also invited to visit Washington if they wished. Such invitations, however, made clear that this land, long occupied by the different tribes, was now the property of the United States.

Chapter 5:
The Long Road Home

Surviving the next few months proved to be at least as difficult as any previous obstacle. Crossing the different mountain ranges exposed them to **frostbite** and **dehydration**. Food was often scarce, and the only thing they had in abundance was freezing temperatures. But whether through luck or skill or a combination of the two, no member of the Corps died.

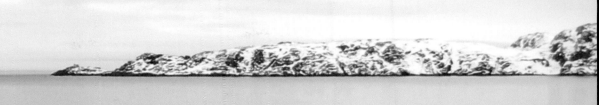

After finally reaching the Pacific Ocean, the
Corps had another hard winter spent near the
site of the future Astoria, Oregon. In the spring of
1806, they were able to head for home. But it was
another six months of travel, trade, and hardship
before the expedition finally reached St. Louis on
September 23.

Lewis and Clark received a hero's welcome upon their return. And certainly they had accomplished a great deal. Perhaps the most valuable of their results were the detailed maps of the 8,000 miles (12,875 km) their journey had covered. Clark's drawings showed the course of rivers and streams, the length of mountain ranges, and the likely spots for settlements in the future. They had not been able to find the much-desired Northwest Passage that would connect the

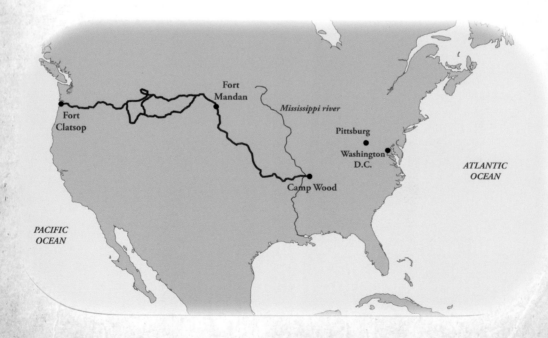

Missouri River with the Pacific Ocean. However, in fairness to their efforts, this passageway did not actually exist.

Among their scientific advances, the explorers had identified over 100 new animals, among them the grizzly bear and the prairie dog. There were even more new plants to be catalogued, including the tumbling **sagebrush** and the towering Ponderosa pines.

Meriwether Lewis and William Clark were both honored for their achievements on behalf of the American people. Lewis was soon named governor of the Louisiana Territory, but it became unclear if he enjoyed the give and take of political life. On October 11, 1809, he died while staying in a tavern near Nashville, Tennessee.

William Clark married Julia Hancock in 1808, and they had a son they named Meriwether Lewis Clark. Later appointed governor of the Missouri Territory, Clark gained a reputation for dealing fairly with the Native American tribes and lived on until September 1, 1838.

While Lewis and Clark may have gone their separate ways after they returned home, their names have remained joined by time. The two men will be forever linked for their remarkable leadership, grit, and determination in leading the most famous expedition in American history.

The Lewis & Clark Monument in Frontier Park, St Charles, Missouri, USA

Glossary

chronometer: An instrument that measures accurate time despite motion or changes in the weather.

dehydration: A condition caused by a lack of water and other fluids

expanse: A vast area of land or water

frostbite: An injury to skin, especially the nose, fingers, and toes, from lengthy exposure to intense cold

gnats: Small, two-winged flies

Indigenous: Describes the first inhabitants of a place

negotiated: Arranged or agreed to after a discussion

portage: To carry a boat and supplies overland for the purpose of continuing a journey between two areas of water

sagebrush: A small, scrubby plant with a strong spicy smell

sextant: An instrument use to measure distance, especially for establishing altitude

Index

Comprehension Questions

What was the goal of the Corps of Discovery?

In what ways did Sacagawea assist Lewis and Clark's expedition?

Why were the maps drawn by Lewis and Clark so valuable?

About the Author

Stephen Krensky is the award-winning author of more than 150 fiction and nonfiction books for children. He and his wife Joan live in Lexington, Massachusetts, and he happily spends as much time as possible with his grown children and not-so-grown grandchildren.

Written by: Stephen Krensky
Designed by: Rhea Wallace
Series Development: James Earley
Proofreader: Janine Deschenes
Educational Consultant: Marie Lemke M.Ed.
Print Coordinator: Katherine Berti

Photo credits: Zack Frank : cover background; Everett Collection: cover, p. 1, 2; Photographs in the Carol M. Highsmith Archive,: p. 6; ZakZeinert: p. 8; Everett Collection: p. 9; Jimmy Emerson, DVM: p. 10; The Granger Collection: p. 11; Everett Collection: p. 12; MidoSemsem: p. 13; Joseph Sohm: p. 15; vagabond54: p. 17; North Wind Picture Archives: p. 18; TTphoto: p. 19; mol_farius: p. 21; LOC: p. 22; Media Whale Stock: p. 24; Dimitrios Karamitros: p. 26; Kristi Blokhin: p. 27; Malachi Jacobs: p. 29

Crabtree Publishing

crabtreebooks.com   800-387-7650
Copyright © 2023 Crabtree Publishing

Printed in the U.S.A./012023/CG20220815

Published in Canada
Crabtree Publishing
616 Welland Ave.
St. Catharines, Ontario
L2M 5V6

Published in the United States
Crabtree Publishing
347 Fifth Ave
Suite 1402-145
New York, NY 10016

Library and Archives Canada Cataloguing in Publication
Available at Library and Archives Canada

Library of Congress Cataloging-in-Publication Data
Available at the Library of Congress

Hardcover: 978-1-0398-0010-6
Paperback: 978-1-0398-0069-4
Ebook (pdf): 978-1-0398-0188-2
Epub: 978-1-0398-0128-8